# Love *or* HATRED

# Love or Hatred

## DAVID WILGUS

THE REGENCY
PUBLISHERS

Copyright © 2022 David Wilgus.

All rights reserved. No part of this book may be reproduced in any form or by any electronic or mechanical means, including information storage and retrieval systems, without permission in writing from the author and publisher, except by reviewers, who may quote brief passages in a review.

ISBN:  978-1-959434-76-4  (Paperback Edition)
ISBN:  978-1-959434-77-1  (Hardcover Edition)
ISBN:  978-1-959434-75-7  (E-book Edition)

Book Ordering Information

The Regency Publishers, International
7 Bell Yard London WO2A2JR

info@theregencypublishers.com
www.theregencypublishers.international
+44 20 8133 0466

Printed in the United States of America

My name is Dave Wilgus.

The story I am about to share with you has weighed heavy on my heart.

The question I will bring to you comes from the event that took place in the state of Minnesota in the year 2021.

The needless killing of a man has been the question the American people have asked; Why the assault?

I am not writing the book "Love or Hatred" to offer an opinion on the subject. My only desire is to inspire the reader by sharing the idea of forgiveness with fellow man.

You, the reader, are about to embark on a journey of two events that have greatly affected our lives today.

The shake, rattle, and roll era had bridged the gap between the "50s and the "60s."

Our nation licked its wounds from the devastation and loss of life because of Japan and Germany. U.S. politicians were the only winners. Power and greed prevailed.

College campuses across the land joined in protest by creating a group known as the "flower children," which opposed violence and supported open sex.

One half million people gathered for a musical concert to speak against the government's wealth priorities. The U. S. and the Kremlin battled to see who would pin their arm to the table first. So they invested significant sums of money into a space race to see who would be the winner of having the first man walk on the moon.

President John F. Kennedy, Civil Rights leader Martin Luther King, and Senator Robert Kennedy were victims of murder.

# WE SHALL OVERCOME

The march to a state capitol and unpopular police action against an Asian people brought the American people to anarchy. The latter brought reports of flag burning and men crossing their northern border to avoid military obligations. The discrimination against people of a different color or ethnic background resulted in turmoil and chaos. It spread through the country like a forest fire.

In the rural area of Stocker, Ohio, stood an abandoned barn covered by fallen trees and swallowed up by weeds and underbrush. The barn bore an eerie notion of being haunted, and the path leading to the barn had empty beer bottles and woman's lingerie. Three boys saw a body suspended from a beam but found only a rope and a remnant's of a man's shirt. Law enforcement probed the report, but they stopped the investigation.

Rumors had leaked out in the community of a group of people gathered for the express purpose of speaking out on "White Supremacy."

A man donned in a white robe and a hooded mask to shield his identity came from the back of the platform. He carried an American flag and walked to the podium to address the crowd.

The noise of cheers and clapping from the audience sounded like a train in the night.

"I welcome you men and women who realize God is supreme and he has a cause for us. So many have heard of what happened to our brothers and sisters in Alabama. We're living in a land of injustice. There is no one better to witness it than my guest from the great state of Alabama.

Please welcome our guest, The Grand Wizard of Alabama."

A man climbed up the stairs from behind the grandstand and walked to greet the host with a spring in his step. His garment of red sported a glittered pattern of stars across each shoulder, and the cone he wore had golden circles of stars embroidered from the hat's brim to the peak.

He joined the man with the flag at the podium, and they shook hands

The crowd went crazy with cheering and fist-pumping into the dark air of the night.

"Hello, my fellow members from Ohio." the wizard announced.

A young man named Chad Henderson had come to the rally because of a grudge against black men who had beaten him after school. He sustained permanent eye damage to one of his eyes. He had difficulty seeing the platform, so he climbed a tree to get a better view.

Gunfire sounded in the crowd, and it startled Chad so much he lost his footing. He grabbed another branch in frantic desperation to keep from falling out of the tree.

The wizard raised both hands in the air to quiet the crowd.

"I have come to seek retaliation for those injured. The people did nothing illegal but only wanted a peaceful demonstration.

We will overcome! We will overcome!" the wizard shouted as he raised his clenched fist.

The crowd joined in by shouting and mimicking the wizard.

Chad felt a knot in the pit of his stomach despite how he felt about black people. He decided to leave before the mob became uncontrollable. Chad attempted to step on a lower branch of the tree when his flashlight fell to the ground. In haste, he leaped out of the tree and retrieved his light. He walked down the path toward the road when he realized the light would not work. Chad visually inspected it and tapped it against his thigh. A sigh of relief came over Chad as the light began to work again.

A substantial psychological effect took hold on Chad, leaving him broken in spirit and unwilling to accept his faults. He could not surpass the feeling of being rejected by people and attempted to overcome vengeance by trying to hurt all blacks. The walk down the lane brought cold shivers up his back. He paused momentarily to listen for noise coming from the rally. However, Chad could only hear faint noises and continued walking. The light beams from the flashlight swayed back and forth until suddenly taillights were illuminated. A man with a full beard and eyes of fire appeared in Chad's path. He had been hiding behind a wood-grained station wagon.

"Who might you be, you wretch," the hermit asked with flaring nostrils. "Quick, give me your name."

"My name is Chad Henderson, sir," trembling with fear.

"You better not speak to anyone about what you witnessed tonight, boy!

"Be gone with you now," snarled the old man.

Chad began to run down the side of the highway in terror.

The town of Stocker believed they lived in an ordinary place. They had the main street, a bench in front of the barbershop, and a fire truck sounding a blast on the siren daily, which turned heads, but the community harbored a hatred for anyone with darker skin.

Chad Henderson, one would say, lived on the wrong side of the tracks. Yet, he had a chip on his shoulder, daring anyone to try and knock it off. Yet, he grew up in a house with his younger brother, Mike, who both boys heard continual fighting between their parents.

His father, an alcoholic and womanizer, and Mary Chad's mother would never have won Parents of the Year awards. After violence escalated, his father abandoned the family. They were divorced when Chad turned twelve, and his mother began a lifestyle of promiscuity after the parting. Chad lived a life of hell with men visiting his house all night.

Chad dropped out of school at seventeen years old. Larry Ardent, a friend of Chad's, had a similar home life. They despised negroes.

Larry dropped out of school in January for no reason other than to sow his wild oats. He landed a job detailing cars at Dinks filling station. Larry managed to locate a cheap apartment but could only meet the rent with Chad's help. Larry's boss agreed to bring Chad on to pump gas during the weekends.

The town of Stocker offered no social life to a teenager, so when the annual Culver High School dance commenced on the last Friday in May, tickets were in high demand.

The class of "65" hosted the dance and the valedictorian happened to be a girl named Cindy Miller.

Larry wanted to go. He had a sweetheart in the eleventh grade named Alice, and he had not seen her for a week.

"Chad, Friday night, there is a dance at the high school. Want to go?"

"I can't dance. I would make a fool of myself."

"Hey, girls are going to be there. My girlfriend will be there."

Of course, Chad could not go up to a stranger and ask them to dance, but there did not seem to be a better alternative for the night.

The gym had a complete make-over with the emcee's podium at north end and refreshments at the south end. Above the large dance floor in the center stage hung a large fishnet suspended with colorful balloons.

Chad and Larry's eyes captured sight of the punchbowl and a cookie table guarded by a couple of adults in formal wear. The boys stood munching on the sweets as their heads rotated like periscopes surveying the girls. Finally, Larry spotted Alice entering the gym and walked over to greet her. Cindy, the host speaker, entered from behind a curtain. She was dressed in a pink gown and wore a pearl necklace drooping across her partially exposed chest. A band member joined her at center stage and handed a microphone to her.

Chad's curiosity perked up as the emcee flashed a smile at him. He countered and walked to the stage.

"Are you ready to kick off the dance?" she shouted.

"Okay, let's kick it off with Chubby Checker and "The Twist."

The crowd roared.

Chad mustered the nerve to attract her attention by waving his hands. She knelt before him, conscious of not exposing her vital anatomy,

"My name is Chad. Will you dance with me?"

Her eyes sparkled in delight as she replied, "yes."

"Be right down after this song."

She gestured to the lead singer to play a slow dance and walked down the stairs to the dance floor. She paused and gazed at the man. He wore tight-fitting jeans, an unkempt T-shirt, and a pack of cigarettes on his sleeve.

"Before I make a fool of myself," Chad said apologetically, "I've never danced before."

"That is okay; I requested a slow song; "I am in heels."

"My name is Cindy Miller," what did you say your name was?"

"The name is Chad, Chad Henderson."

He took her into his arms, and a spark of warmth bonded them.

Cindy giggled as she wrapped her arms tighter around his waist and pressed against Chad's solid frame.

"Chad, Are you still in school? I haven't seen you in the hallways."

"No," Chad replied, Trying his best not to step on her feet.

"I never did well in school. So I live with a friend, and he is getting me a job at a gas station."

"Where do you live?"

"I live on Farnell Street. Can I ask you a question?"

She didn't reply, but pushed him away as the music stopped.

The night drug on as the music played. He returned to the refreshment stand and dreamt of Cindy being his wife.

"Listen up, the last dance of the night. "It Hurts to Be in Love," so grab your partner. Then, as quick words came out of her mouth, she disappeared behind a curtain near the back of the stage.

Chad scurried behind the platform with an irritable grunt and intercepted Cindy heading for the exit.

A vague fear came over Cindy's face.

"I wanted to ask you if I could see you again?"

"I better not; I have a jealous boyfriend."

He turned away, feeling sad and broken.

"Wait a minute; he has asked me to marry him. I do not love him, and I am afraid of him. Give me time, and I will try and get rid of him. Give me your phone number or address, and I will contact you."

Chad's eyes became as bright as the reflection of sunlight on a stream.

His hands shook like a moth caught in a lampshade as he wrote down his address on a piece of paper.

Saturday morning, Cindy received a phone call from her boyfriend, Bill. He asked if she would go with him to Brewer's malt shop. She decided it would be the best time and place to send him packing out of her life, so she agreed.

Twenty minutes later, an old beater screeched to a halt behind Cindy's house. The car needed a coat of paint, and the driver did not look any better. He met Cindy halfway up the driveway and began making excuses on why he did not make it to the dance.

He pulled up in front of the malt shop and leaped out of the car without opening the door.

Once inside, Cindy slid into a booth near the door in case she had to escape.

Bill sat across from her and craned his head toward her for a kiss, but she declined his offer.

"Is that any way to act toward me?"

Cindy shrugged her shoulders. She knew how this date would end, but she wanted to vent her feelings and get on with her life.

A familiar face approached their booth.

"What you guys want?"

Darlene dressed in a skirt barely reaching her knees and a laced blouse had been a fixture since the malt shop opened.

Cindy asked for a vanilla milkshake, and Bill ordered a vanilla coke.

Darlene did an about-face wiggling her hips as she strolled back to the counter with their order.

"I have great news. I start a new job on Monday at a filling station. It will pay three dollars an hour, and we can afford to get married and get an apartment with that kind of money I make."

Cindy noticed that Miss Flaunty was approaching with the glasses in her peripheral vision, so she delayed her response.

Darlene placed the drinks on the table, tore the invoice out of her tablet, and laid it on the table.

Cindy reached for a straw from the dispenser and tore the paper off. Then, she plunged the straw into the shake like she was trying to hit an imaginary bullseye. Then, with eyes focused on the shake, she raised her head like a cobra popping its head out of a basket and said, "Bill, I do not love you, and I won't marry you."

A red shade began to radiate on his neck, like a thermometer placed in a boiling pot of fudge. He raised his fist and brought it down on the table, striking his Coke glass's side, spilling it all over the table.

"Who is he? What is his name?"

"It has nothing to do with it; I do not love you!"

"I do not know who he is, but when I find out, he will wish he were never born!"

She hurried off the bench like a hot knife going through butter and turned to leave, but Bill grabbed her arm. She jerked her arm from his grasp and ran out of the shop.

Before he could pay the bill, Cindy disappeared.

Willie Crawford's arrest was broadcast three weeks later on Stocker's radio station. Cindy sighed when she heard of Willie Crawford's arrest.

Cindy's mother, Verna, did not like Chad as soon as she met him. She had a controlling personality since the loss of her husband to cancer. Mr. Miller had a prestigious job in a pharmaceutical company, and Verna became dependent upon him. She felt threatened by anyone who would come between Cindy and her. Chad overlooked Verna's controlling nature, and after six months of dating, Chad and Cindy were married.

With the aid of Cindy's mom's financing, the newlyweds could buy a quaint three-bedroom home on the outskirts of Stocker.

Chad began a new job at a foundry making engine parts. America was reaching a peak in manufacturing products and goods primarily because of the war in Vietnam. To be unemployed at this time would be non-existent. Chad's future at work looked promising. He was starting on the ground floor, and there was room for advancement.

In January of 1966, Cindy and Chad welcomed their first child into the world. A baby girl who weighed five pounds nine ounces. Their marriage union and the addition of Brooke should have strengthened their commitment to one another, but anxiety hung over them like a dark impenetrable cloud. Each held a dark secret. Cindy never shared the threat her ex-boyfriend had made on Chad's life. She knew someday Bill would get out of jail but would not believe Bill would follow through on the harm he wanted to inflict on Chad.

Chad had his own skeletons in his closet. In retaliation for a black boy's assault in high school, he sought an opportunity to get revenge."

Chad got involved with a band of people whose beliefs promoted "White Supremacy." However, his very solution released the hatred that overwhelmed his soul.

Monday morning began with the menacing sound of the alarm clock signaling time to start a new week. Two months into his new job, it had become a boring way of life for him to get up early every morning to go to work.

Cindy usually got up each morning to fix him breakfast and pack his lunch, but because they got to bed so late, he gathered his clothes, tip-toed out of the bedroom, and dressed in the bathroom. To his surprise, when he came out of the bathroom and met Cindy.

"Why didn't you wake me?"

"I thought you were asleep." Chad replied with a sympathetic response.

She grasped him by the waist and kissed him passionately. "Do not be silly-I love you."

"My job is to wait on you because I love you."

A radiant look came over his face like a ray of sudden sunshine on a cloudy day. Chad followed Cindy to the kitchen with the headlong zest of a hunter after his game.

"There is lunchmeat in the fridge if you want to make your lunch today."

"Chad, can I ask you a question?"

He walked over behind her and placed his arms around her waist.

"What is on your mind, baby?"

She turned as he lost his grip on her waist.

"Would you be willing to start going to church as a family?"

"I do not know. I work all week and the weekends are the only time I can relax."

She turned back to the stove and finished flipping the last flapjack.

They sat at the table eating the pancakes as silence overshadowed the room. Then, finally, Chad jumped up from his chair and scampered to the door.

"What is the matter with you?"

"I am going to be late for work. Quick, kiss me."

He ran halfway to the truck and stopped dead in his tracks. Cindy stood in the doorway with his keys dangling on her finger. He ran back to her and snatched the keys from her grasp and kissed her again.

The motor cranked a few times before firing up, and he rolled down the window.

"I will try and call you on my lunch break."

As he neared the railroad tracks, the warning lights began to flash.

I was caught by a train! *I will be late now. What will I tell the boss?*

He sat hypnotized watching the wheels rolling on the tracks. Then, finally, the last car passed, and the gates began to rise. His engine revved up causing the rear wheels to kick up stones. Chad arrived ten minutes late, and the supervisor stood positioned near the clock, ready for a confrontation with Chad.

"Glad you could make it, Henderson," the boss smirked in a sarcastic scowl.

Chad never responded but instead positioned himself at his stamping press. The clanging of metal striking metal would be more soothing to his ears than to hear the guff from the supervisor, "Barking Bob," as they called him.

A ragged man worked near Chad. He was a broad man with a receding hairline and a gray beard.

Chad was like a magnet for those who people less accepted. Junior Bradley, the youngest of two boys, had been abandoned by his father when he was young. His mother raised him the best she could but he had a speech problem that hampered his ability to fit in with people. At sixteen, he dropped out of school, stole a man's car, then robbed a beer joint. He served a two to five stretch for grand theft and robbery. Junior operated a drill press all day, slamming steel pins into a metal flange that would send a high pitch noise throughout the shop.

The whistle blew, and Chad stripped his gloves off and slammed them down on his table.

"Well c Chad, what is bothering you. You can trust me."

"Nothing, Junior, let's go over to the table and eat our lunch."

Junior followed Chad like a timid sheep to the slaughter. However, he had great respect for Chad, and he looked up to him as a brother.

"It is Cindy and me. We are having problems at home."

"I aa lmost got married once. Its w worked out best we did not."

"CCchad, how about we s stop after work for a c cold one?"

"Sure, but just one, I must get home."

"Cindy would not be happy with me if she suspected me of drinking, and besides, I have trouble stopping with just one."

The last whistle of the day was like a refreshing rain on dusty grass.

Chad and Junior raced to the clock like two men running a marathon in the Olympics.

Dixie's happened to be a sanctuary for even the casual drinker. Where else could you find good old red neck music, a cold beer, and wild women? Also, it had two pool tables and every week had shuffle-board tournaments.

For Junior, it was a home away from home.

Monday nights were like a hornet's nest with servers running around serving the "all you can-eat Walleye."

"What can I get you men?"

"Two beers, ordered Junior."

"Two dollars," as he popped the caps off the bottled and placed them in front of the men. They grabbed the beers and walked over to a table near the jukebox.

The bottles were drunk like sand going into a sinkhole.

Chad walked back up to the bar and bought two more beers.

"Junior, it is time for me to go home and face the music. See you tomorrow."

"Good luck Chad; I don't wish anyone to face the music you will face."

# A NEW BEGINNING

The potential disaster would be a cinch if Chad did not remember to stop at the market to get something for dinner. So away he rushed into the store and then drew a blank.

*What do I get? If I get something cooked, it will go better for me. So I will buy some fried chicken and potato salad. That will work.*

It was now 5:30, and he knew Cindy would be worried about his delay. He hoped the chicken would do the trick. They had been married for two years, and Cindy had tolerated his drinking like a woman who enjoys a broken leg. Chad made the turn into his driveway and struck the trash can, which stood by the end of the driveway.

He exited the truck with Cindy standing in the doorway with her hands on her hips and shaking her head in animosity.

"Have you been drinking again? "

"It was hot in that shop. I just had a couple. I did not harm anybody."

"That trash can could have been another car, Chad!"

"You are right, honey. But I brought home some chicken."

"It will not work; we ate an hour ago," Cindy said, with a stain of irritability in her voice.

Cindy marched to her bedroom and slammed the door rattling the photo on the wall.

Chad made his way to his easy chair and reached for the newspaper off the end table. The opening of the bedroom door heightened Chad's senses as he speculated Cindy would be poking a finger into his face like a ravening lunatic.

"I am going to bed," came the irritating response. Cindy slammed the door again.

Three o'clock in the morning, and labor pains began.

"It is time to go to the hospital. Get Brooke in the car, and I will call Mom."

Chad rushed to the bathroom door and stopped. He had been in such a deep sleep that he had not realized what she had said.

"You mean it's the time!"

"Yes, ninny. It's time." smiled Cindy.

Verna stood in the driveway when Chad entered the driveway.

"Chad, as she opened the back door, give me a call and let me know what is going on, okay?"

"Okay, Mom, I will call you as soon as we know something."

A security guard stood at the hospital entrance when they arrived. He noticed Chad's panic. He went into the foyer and brought out a wheelchair.

Forty-five minutes later, Joshua could be heard crying in the hallway.

Joshua tipped the scale at three pounds, nine ounces, and thirteen inches long. The date: November 13, 1967. Joshua seemed healthy but would have to stay in the hospital until he gained weight.

Ten miles south of Stocker housed a community of migrant negro workers. In the early 1700's a man named Howard Brigsley, a sympathizer for runaway slaves, settled the town of Brigsley. The group of people could save enough money to build a school and church, but for fuel and supplies, they had to depend on a bigot and scoundrel, Nelson Fisk. He was a festering sore which would not scab over.

Fisk's market, the last stop before getting to the community of Brigsly, left all the people at the tyrant's mercy.

Two of Fisk's bodyguards, Jeb Townsend and Henry Burke, took residence on the front porch. One would think their purpose was to hold down a chair and push red and black checkers on a burlap checkerboard. There had been a day when each man had a family, but like Fisk, they were troublesome.

Henry, a cantankerous man, lost his farm during the depression. A blind rage like a fire swept over him one day, so he took his frustrations out on his family. He returned from work to find his hidden tobacco pouch emptied of his money.

Townsend fell out of grace with his dad when he refused to work on the farm.

The Ohio North Central railroad hired him as a switch operator. He dressed the part of a railroad worker wearing bib overalls and sporting a red handkerchief out his back pocket. He claimed he hurt his back while at work; however, fellow workers would not corroborate his story, and the railroad terminated him.

Amos Parsons, a soft-spoken negro with higher education than the average negro in Brigsley, came from Mississippi in 1960.

Millie, the love of his life, and their eight-year-old daughter Becky lived in a single home north of Brigsley. As the people of Brigsley Baptist Church called Mr Parson's to be their elder.

A visit to Fisk's market would be the last thing Amos would have chosen, but he needed gas and medication for Becky's headache.

Fisk sat near the store's front door, reading the newspaper, when the ding of the bell rang, signaling a customer was at the gas pump.

Hey Willie, didn't you hear the bell!" hollered Fisk.

"I heard the bell, shouted Willie. I can only be in one place at one time," as he entered the store from the alley behind the store.

He angrily knocked over a sign on display when he pushed through the store's front door.

"Don't rush Willie, Jeb replied, as the men studied Amos standing by his black sedan.

One night, Willie Crawford met Fisk at Dixie's bar and he gave Fisk a hard luck story. Unfortunately, Fisk had a couple of drinks, so he gave Crawford a job and provided him with a musty old room in the back of the store.

Willie looked at Jeb and Henry with cold eyes and proceeded to step off the porch. The boy loved any chance to provoke someone into a fight. He received many a beating by his old man while living at home so being a bully for him was second nature.

"What can I do for you, boy?" he snarled at Amos.

Amos looked over the roof of his car in the direction of the voice.

"I need a dollar worth of fuel."

Willie took the gas nozzle from the pump, the gas cap off, and jammed the nozzle into the gas inlet.

Amos gave him a dirty look but thought it better to leave well enough alone. He walked up the stairs onto the top landing and noticed one of the men nearest the door scooting his chair to his left to prohibit Amos from opening the screen door.

"I don't want any trouble, sir!"

Jeb reluctantly lifted his chair back to the right enabling him to open the door.

The next hurdle would be the hardest-Nelson Fisk.

Fisk captured Parson's eye as he pushed through the screen door.

"What's your name," asked Fisk.

"Amos Parsons."

"Okay, get what you want and get out!"

Amos shrugged and walked down each aisle till he found the medicine.

He took a bottle of medicine off the top shelf.

He turned to look at the menacing figure standing behind the cash register. A chill ran down his spine as he walked to the front of the store. He sat the bottle on the counter in front of Fisk.

"That will be ninety-nine cents plus a dollar for the gas."

"The price on the bottle reads fifty-nine cents," Amos shouted back. He pulled a dollar from his wallet and fifty-nine cents from his pocket and placed them on the counter. Parson picked up the medicine and turned towards the door, but Fisk grabbed his arm.

Amos Parson, a God-fearing man, tried to avoid altercations with his fellow man, but Fisk had pushed him to his limit. He drew back his fist and hit the old codger driving him into a display of cigarettes on the back counter. Packs of smokes flew into the air and onto the floor.

Fisk let out a blood-curdling scream as the blood gushed from his nose.

The two men on the front porch jumped out of their chairs and looked through the screen door. Amos pushed through the door and raised his fist in case the man wanted to hit him.

Amos stepped down onto the first step of the porch and felt a blow to the back of his head. He rolled down to the bottom of the stairs, knocked unconscious.

"You're in big trouble, boy," said Fisk, not realizing the man had been knocked unconscious.

"Somebody call an ambulance," yelled Townsend as he knelt by Amos' limp body.

Parson's attempted to get to his feet when he heard sirens in the distance.

"You better stay down on your face, nigger, if you know what's good for you!"

A Stocker police cruiser and an ambulance arrived on the scene. The paramedics helped Amos get into a chair.

Sgt. Bill Stone, the senior officer, knew of Fisk's hatred for blacks from previous complaints.

"What's going on here? What happened to the man Fisk?" Stone asked.

"I'll tell you what's going on!" Fisk shouted. The man tried to leave without paying me all money due to me!"

"What's your name?" asked Stone.

"My name is Amos Parsons. And I did not cheat anybody."

Amos reached into his pocket, pulled out the medicine bottle, and handed it to Stone.

"Look at the price on the bottle. He tried to charge me ninety-nine cents when it reads fifty-nine cents. So I paid the man fifty-nine cents, and he grabbed my arm, so I hit him."

"He has a point, Nelson; he hit you in self-defense. However, the bottle reads fifty-nine cents, so I think you would be wise to return to the store and forget it."

"Okay, but I won't forget it! I will get even for what he did!" Saturday morning, a phone call woke Chad. A low-pitched voice came over the phone.

"Hello,"

"Is this Chad Henderson?"

"Why yes, who is this?"

"Never mind who this is. You know the old logging trail out by Hiway 12? Be there at six-thirty tonight. We are going to teach someone a lesson."

"Hello!" Click.

Chad heard the bedroom door creak open.

"Who is on the phone?" asked Cindy.

The color of Chad's face faded away.

"Oh, wrong number."

"But I heard you talking to someone, Chad."

"They asked for someone else. Then hung up."

Cindy slammed the door shut, mumbling under her breath. She knew getting an honest answer would be impossible.

Chad's heart raced all day to think of someone who might get hurt or caught.

"Cindy, do you mind if I go bowling tonight?"

"No, as long as you don't stop for a drink. Who's going with you?"

"I think I will call Junior and ask him to go with me."

Chad kissed Cindy goodbye and took his bowling bag out of the closet.

"Remember what I said, Chad, no drinking."

"I remember, baby."

Chad backed out of the driveway, and his stomach fluttered like a band of bewildered moths caught in a lampshade. Then he drove through the night, passing several cars on the highway. Chad craned his head in the rear-view mirror to see if a red light sat on the roof. As he approached the logging trail intersection, his hands began to squeeze the steering wheel.

An illuminating light swayed back and forth from the left side of the road, and someone stepped out into the street, causing Chad to stop. A figure dressed in a white robe and a cone-shaped hood walked up to Chad's door.

"Wait here till I get you your package. The man walked over to a wood-grain station wagon and lowered the back hatch. He pulled out a brown box and carried it over to Chad.

"Follow down this lane, and someone will give you instructions."

Chad pitched the package to the passenger seat and drove down the lane, passing a line of cars and trucks. Another person dressed in the same costume stood next to the last car and instructed Chad to turn his vehicle around and pull in behind the previous vehicle.

His mind raced with the question of "what-if," and his breathing labored with pain creeping into his chest, but it was too late to turn back.

Time seemed to pass like syrup dripping from a bottle at forty degrees below zero as he waited.

He pondered the possibility of turning in the other direction when the procession turned one way.

The roar of the engines broke the silence and a bright illumination lit the sky.

The procession moved forward inch by inch until they reached the hi-way.

A visible ranch house came into view, and a burning cross lit the night sky in the front yard. The fire seemed to burn brighter. As Chad's truck passed the house, he could see two people kneeling in the yard but could not see what they were doing. Chad grew sick to his stomach.

When the car in front of Chad turned left, Chad turned right, nearly putting his truck in the ditch. He raced home but could hear sirens in the far distance.

*What if they recognize my truck? Could he disguise the guilt once Cindy learned of the assault?*

The house never looked so great once Chad pulled into the driveway. He grabbed the box and the bowling bag and rushed to the garage.

A tall oak cabinet stood next to his workbench, where he hung his greasy work clothes. Chad had built a secret compartment where he sometimes hid his alcohol. He moved the tools out and opened the secret door where he stashed the brown package.

He put everything back into the cabinet and walked back to the garage door.

Chad picked up the bowling bag and scampered to the kitchen door. A sudden sense of fear came over him when he turned the knob of the door and opened it. Cindy's smiling face scared him.

"Hello honey, have a wonderful time?"

"Why yes, I had two good games and one not so good."

"I laid a towel and washrag out for you if you want to take a shower."

"Thanks, I sure need one."

# TROUBLE BREWING

The following day Chad picked up the newspaper on the front porch to see if there were any details on the assault. The dispatch showed a vivid photo of the remnants of a charred cross twenty feet in front of the home of a man named Amos Parson. He sustained severe burns on over forty-five per cent of his body.

The steeple bells rang their joyous melody for a call to worship in the town of Stocker, but another alarm sounded at the home of Chad Henderson on Sunday morning. Cindy heard a car door slamming and went to the front door.

A blue sedan with two men dressed in suits exited the car. The passenger opened the back door and pulled out a brown box.

Cindy stood trembling as she waited for the men to reach the front door.

"May I help you?"

John Romano reached inside his jacket and pulled out a black leather case opened it and flashed it to her-FBI agents.

"My name is Detective John Romano, and my partner, Edward Higgins. Is your husband Chad Henderson home?"

"What's this all about?"

"Don't worry, ma'am, all we want to do is ask him a few questions."

"Yes, he is in the bathroom; why don't you come in."

Cindy led them to the living room and offered them a chair.

They refused the offer and stood looking around the living room.

"Chad, you have company!"

"Okay, I will be right out.?"

He came out, drying his hands with a towel.

The men greeted Chad with a handshake.

"My name is Det. John Romano and Corporal Ed Higgins. We are here to ask you some questions."

"Sure, what's this all about?" Chad asked in a defensive tone.

"Last night on Highway 12, an attack occurred to a family. Do you know anything about it?

"Yes, I read it in today's paper."

Romano stared at Chad in a spirit of frustration; his brow bent like a cliff o'er his thoughts.

"You know this would be much easier if you would tell me the truth."

"What do you mean, mister?"

"We found an empty pasteboard box along the road where the attack occurred, and your name is on the box."

Romano handed the box to Chad to examine.

A look of bewilderment came over Chad and Cindy's faces.

"Recognize it, Mr. Henderson?"

Chad had regret written all over his face. He pondered the box for a moment.

"Yes, I ordered a part for my lawnmower a few days ago and pitched the box in the bed of my truck. The other day, I drove to a friend's house. So it must have blown out."

"Where does your friend live?" asked Higgins

"On 400 North off of Highway 12."

"But 400 North is not near the Parsons's home. So will you have us believe the box flew over three miles and landed in a ditch in front of the Parson's home?"

Cindy stood by Chad's side. But, she knew in her heart he had lied.

"Where were you at 6:00?"

"I went bowling at Suttons Lanes."

"Chad, you might as well tell them the truth. They are going to check your alibi."

The vengeance Chad sought for his past became a mute-point as he began to weep.

"Mr. Henderson, you must come with us for additional questioning. We must put restraints on you for everyone's safety?"

"Where are you taking my husband," Cindy hollered.

"We will be taking him to the jail in Stocker."

The men escorted Chad to their automobile and helped him get in the back seat. Cindy began to cry as the car backed out of the driveway. Cindy lost all hope for her life. The children and their welfare had vanished from her thought process. She had nowhere to turn. A small comfort was a mad dash to her bedroom and a leap on her bed to spill her sorrow.

She went into the kitchen, picked up the phone, and called her mother. She dialed the phone in such a hurry she got the wrong number. She made another attempt as her mind raced.

"Mom, can you come over? It's Chad; he is in jail."

"Yes, I will get there as soon as I can. So what's the matter?"

"I can't explain over the phone."

Cindy fed Joshua while Brooke sat at the kitchen table coloring a picture with crayons. Cindy's mind pondered on whether Chad would go to prison. How would she support the kids? Would she have to get a job? What would people think?

Her thoughts were interrupted when she heard a knock on the front door.

"Wait a minute,"

She put the baby in the crib and raced to the door, with Brooke coming in second.

The picturesque embrace of a daughter and mother set the tone for the insurmountable hill Cindy had to climb.

Cindy wept bitterly on Verna's shoulder while Brooke hugged her mother's leg.

Verna knew silence would be the best help she could offer at the time, but she knew of a man who had counseled people in such situations.

"Cindy, would you consider seeking spiritual guidance?"

"What are you saying, mom?"

"Pastor Keen, the pastor at Victory church, has given spiritual input to help many people. He is personable and not judgmental. Would you mind if I call him?"

Cindy knew her mom's advice was best.

Verna suggested that Cindy lay down while she made the call.

The car door slam interrupted the card game Verna and Brooke was playing.

Verna opened Cindy's bedroom door and told her they were there.

"Okay, mom, I am getting up."

Verna greeted her dear friends at the door and invited them to come into the living room.

"May I get you folks an ice- tea?"

Edna asked if she could have unsweetened.

Verna responded with a nod. Pastor Keen requested ice water.

Verna went to the kitchen while Cindy came from the bedroom.

"Hello, Mr. and Mrs. Keen."

The couple arose from the couch and greeted her.

"Why don't you call us by our first names, Bill and Edna. We want you to be comfortable with us."

Cindy gave out a smile and a sigh of relief.

Verna brought the beverages and placed them on the table in front of Bill and Edna.

Bill began with an opening prayer and then turned to Cindy.

"Okay, Cindy, we are here to listen and support you if you want to begin."

Cindy cradled her head into her hands for a moment and slowly raised her head in the direction of Bill.

She shared the visit by law enforcement and explained their reasons for taking Chad to jail. Cindy paused.

In a sympathetic tone, Bill reassured Cindy of everything shared would be in the highest confidence.

"God is in control of the situation, and we should accept God for His will and outcome. So if you want me to go to the jail and speak to Chad, I would be glad to do it for you?"

Cindy answered with a smile.

The morning had arrived for Cindy to visit the man she had given her love. She sought the answer to why he would do what he did. Fear raced through her mind as she drove to the cage which held her husband captive.

*Should I be compassionate? Should I be angry? Should I support him?*

On the grounds of the building stood "Ole Glory," waving in the breeze with a plaque with the etched words," truth, justice liberty."

Cindy found comfort in the words etched on the memorial.

She walked to a reception desk where an older man sat wearing thick lens glasses.

"May I help you, ma'am?"

"Yes, I am here to visit my husband, Chad Henderson," answered Cindy.

He handed her a register book and told her to sign it. She took the book, trembling, scribbled her name, and then handed it back.

The man pointed to a chair and told her to sit until someone came to get her.

A giant of a woman came through a steel door. Cindy gazed at the woman in shock. She had never seen a woman that big. She asked her to put her hands against the wall.

Cindy complied and cringed when the woman ran her hands up and down her body.

"Follow me," she huffed.

The hallway had dampness in the air; a cold and eerie feeling came over Cindy.

The woman stopped at a steel door, reached for a metal tag on her hip, and slid it into a slot on the door. The clicking sound freed the barred door and gave way to a hallway with a plexus-glass wall with numerous stools. At each seat hung a black phone.

Suddenly, another loud noise came from the other side of the room and a man entered.

Chad walked through the door with a man and told him to go to a stool.

Chad had an scruffy appearance, and a vague fear possessed his face. Finally, he sat down and gestured for Cindy to pick up her phone.

"Hi, honey. I am deeply sorry. Will you forgive me?

"It will take time for me, Chad. What were you thinking?"

Chad lowered his head to avoid eye contact with her.

"Cindy, I know I have not been the husband and father I should have been, but when I get out of this predicament, I will change."

"Does it mean you will start going to church with me?"

"We will talk about that later, okay," Chad answered with a defiant attitude.

On that note, Cindy hung up the phone, stood, and turned to the exit door.

Chad slammed down the phone on the cradle and stood up in rejection.

The interrogation had reached four hours on the second day, and finally, the parties agreed.

Chad would turn state's witness to help with the prosecution.

The state of Ohio assigned a Prosecuting Attorney by the name of Jake Simpson to work with the Federal Agents and handle the investigation. He had a distinct limp from a hip injury suffered in the Vietnam crisis but had no bearing on his intellect and success in prosecuting criminals. He had a reputation for winning the vast majority of his cases.

Romano and Higgins took Chad home, understanding he would turn over the hidden package in the garage.

Cindy stood in the kitchen fixing lunch for Brooke when the blue sedan turned into the driveway.

"Daddy's home, Brooke."

Her thoughts turned to tears like sunshine in the rain. They ran out the door and waited for the agents to release him. Chad climbed out of the car and Cindy lunged at him with her arms securing a tight grasp on his shoulders while Brooke held her arms up for her daddy to pick her up.

He obliged.

"Are you free?"

I am free, but I must take the men to the garage now."

Chad kissed Brooke and handed her back to Cindy.

Romano and Higgins followed Chad into the garage, and he stopped at an oak cabinet.

The men watched Chad's every move as he reached the side of the cabinet and secured a hidden key from under a hanging pipe wrench. One would think a treasure of gold awaited the men in black as Chad opened the lock. But instead, Chad flung the doors open to a wooden box filled with tools and numerous auto parts.

"Give me a hand pulling the box out," asked Chad.

He gave way to the men, and they slid the box out onto the floor.

Chad opened the secret door in the cabinet and handed the package to Romano.

Romano stepped back from the cabinet and stared briefly at the wrapped package. Romano knew what he would be opening would go far in prosecuting the culprits who injured Parsons. So he opened it and found two garments tightly wrapped. A cone-shaped hood and the other piece was a white robe with the letters: "Nucleus Inc." on the hem of the garment.

Romano smiled.

# A DEADLY MISTAKE

The ding of the elevator signaled the door to open. Millie Parsons stepped out into a dorm of the burn unit. Curtains were visible and suspended from metal tracks with no nurses in view. A tear slid down Millie's cheek as she pondered what the future would bring. Then, the touch of a hand on her shoulder brought her mind back to the reason for her visit.

"First time on a burn unit, ma'am? came a voice from behind her.

"Yes, it is," as she turned around. I am here to visit my husband, Amos Parsons."

A middle-aged woman stood with a warm smile, dressed in a blue smock and a stethoscope hanging around her neck.

"Oh, yes, please follow me, Mrs. Parsons."

She led her to the third curtain on the right and stopped. The nurse pulled back the curtain so Millie could peek in. The horror of Amos lying wrapped like a mummy brought trembling to Millie's body.

"Wait here, and I will get you a chair."

Millie looked at her husband in disbelief.

*Is it a dream? I cannot believe what I am seeing. If only Anos would not have gotten near the fire.*

The noise of the nurse entering through the curtain with the chair brought Millie out of her dream.

"Here, Mrs. Parsons, you may sit down. Dr. Fitzgerald will be making his rounds soon. May I get you something to drink?"

She sat clutching her purse and squeezing the purse straps aggressively.

A response never came. Millie sat and began to pray for her husband of ten years would survive the trauma to his body, and her mind drifted off again.

*A cross represents love, so why is it used for hatred? Christ died for all men.*

As far back as she could remember, a God-fearing woman had suffered a life of persecution because of her skin color. But when she met Amos, her life had new meaning.

After their marriage, the couple migrated north at the request of Parson Zebadiah Lindstrom of Mount Zion Church.

Millie gave birth in 1961 to a daughter named Rebecca, after Millie's mother, Rebecca Stone.

Once again, the silence broke with the entry of a tall man sporting a white coat with gray peppered hair. He reached out his hand to Millie, and she clutched his hand.

"My name is Dr. Clarence Fitzgerald. Your husband has sustained severe injuries. He lost two fingers on his left hand and one on his right. In addition, your husband has suffered extensive burns to his face. We found unknown foreign plastic particles attached to his skin. We are sending skin samples to our toxicology lab to determine why there is so much damage to his skin. Unfortunately, I cannot give you a period on how long he will be a patient, but we are doing our best.

Millie never said anything but got up from her chair, left the room, and headed for the elevator.

Chad returned to work the next day with great anxiety regarding what his co-workers might ask him. Chad sensed Junior wanted to speak but held his tongue.

The thought of explaining his reasons was personal and nobody's business. As Chad reached across to grab his iced tea, he accidentally knocked over a box of fasteners sending them to the floor. The box opened and screws went in every direction. He bent down and began picking up the spill when a black boot came close to stepping on his hand.

"Let me help you."

Chad looked up to identify the familiar voice.

Junior had been the best friend anyone could ever want. He found an empty box on a workbench, squatted down, and began scooping the stock up with his hands.

"Well, I suppose you heard what happened, Junior?"

"Yeah, C chad, but only what I read in the papers. You have a lawyer?"

"No, I won't need one. Everything will work out."

"What do you mean by that, C chad?"

"Please, Junior, I do not want to talk about it anymore; why don't we stop at Dixie's after work, and I will talk then."

"Okay, C chad."

A man in trouble does not always turn to the apparent person to share his problems. Such is the case with Chad. Instead, he turned to the only friend he believed he had, Junior.

The men met at Dixie's as planned and found a secluded table. The waitress approached them, chewing vigorously on a wad of gum.

"What will you have, men?"

"Beers, Junior responded, holding up two fingers.

The waitress left and returned with the drinks, picked up the money, and went to another table where two men had sat down within earshot of Chad and Junior. Chad focused his attention on the men as the waitress took their order. He noticed the logo "Nucleus Inc." on the back of one of the men's shirts.

"What is the matter, Chad?"

"I thought I had seen the man who is seated near us. Forget it Junior, I am not feeling well; I think I will go home. I am truly sorry. See you tomorrow at work, okay?"

"Sure, buddy, "Junior replied.

Chad walked to the door and took another look at the men.

Junior noticed two men shooting pool and decided to challenge the winner. He placed a quarter on the rim of the pool table, signifying his intent. The game ended, and the loser put his cue into the holder mounted on the wall.

Crowley Denton watched patiently for Junior to finish his turn, then grabbed his beer and got up from his chair.

"Excuse me, but I need you to come to my table so I can ask you some questions," Denton said roughly.

"I am busy shooting pool," replied Junior.

"Listen, dummy; I am telling you to finish the game and then get over to my table!"

Junior raised his cue and swung it, hitting Denton across his face and causing the beer Denton held to crash onto the floor. Martin raced out the door behind several patrons. A few people stood to enjoy the brawl. Denton and Junior exchanged blows, but most of Denton's jabs missed Junior. Denton and Junior wrestled across the floor when Denton pulled out a knife from his boot and made a thrust at Junior, slashing him in the arm. Junior grasped his bleeding arm but seized the chance to dislodge the blade from Denton's hand. Denton got up from the floor but not before an unknown man hid in the crowd plunged a knife into Junior's side. The man rose from the floor and seemed to disappear into thin air.

"Call an ambulance," came a cry from patrons as Junior began to turn blue.

Barney the owner of the tavern grabbed towels from the counter under the bar and rushed to the wounded man. He knelt at his side, trying to limit the loss of blood.

The police and ambulance arrived simultaneously. Medics rushed through the doors with the gurney and placed oxygen mask on Junior while the other man set up an IV for Junior.

"Okay, everyone back and gives us the room."

"What on earth happened here?" hollered Sergeant Stone.

Barney Ginter, the bartender, stepped from the crowd and motioned Stone to follow him to the bar.

"Okay, Barney, what happened?"

Stone fired one question after another. *Finally, the bartender testified the two men at the table as men who would often come in on the Friday night fish fry. One of the men wore a shirt with the insignia; "Nucleus Inc" on the back of his shirt. His name is Crowly Denton. He started a fight with the man stabbed. Another man with long hair and a checkered shirt knelt by the man's body on the floor, then stood up and went back into the crowd.*

"Where did he go?" the Sergeant asked.

"He vanished after he got back in the crowd."

"Corporal Burgess is it okay to take him now?" asked one of the medics.

"Okay, Bud, take some pictures so the medics can get him out of here."

"Get out of the way and make a path," yelled one of the medics.

The men rushed him to the ambulance and sped off to the hospital.

Chad returned to work, as usual, unaware of Junior's altercation.

Thursday morning, Chad returned to the timeclock and the grim-looking supervisor, "Barking Bob."

He reached the worktable he had been chained to since eternity began but to his shock; the day did not start as he had planned. Instead, at Junior's worktable, stood a man who had a beard and wore a red scarf about his neck.

"Who are you," Chad yelled out in defense of Junior.

"My friends call me Jonesy, and I do not like your tone of voice!"

"Sorry, buddy, I am not used to seeing anyone else there but Junior."

"Who in blazes is this man Junior you say?"

Chad turned in panic to locate Barking Bob.

He stood at his desk shuffling through papers.

"Hey Bob, can I talk to you?" Chad pleaded.

In disgust, Bob laid the papers on the desk and went to Chad's beckoning.

"What you need, Henderson?"

"Where is Junior, sick?"

"He is more than sick; He is in the hospital fighting for his life."

A face of stone would be best to describe Chad. His mind flashed back to the night before at Dixie's. *He reminisced the sight of the tight shirt worn by the man at the table. How did the connection between Junior with the guy come about? Could the attack have been meant for him?*

Chad called Cindy during his lunch break about what had happened to Junior and his desire to visit the hospital after work. Unfortunately, the shift could not end fast enough for Chad.

A hospital is for the welfare of the ill but not a place to visit. Chad could only remember going to the hospital when Brooke and Joshua were born. His stomach turned in knots as he entered the parking lot. He parked and sat momentarily in the car, gathering his thoughts before he got out of the truck.

He approached the hospital entrance and a security guard greeted him.

"May I help you, sir:"

"I am here to see my friend."

The guard turned and faced the entrance door.

"Go through these doors, and the lady in red can help you."

Chad obeyed and paused to let a woman out the door in a wheelchair.

"May I help you, sir?"

"Yes, I am here to see a friend. His name is Bill Bradley?"

"The room number is twenty seven."

"Thank you, ma'am."

Chad counted the numbers on the doors under his breath and came to room 27. He took a deep breath. The fear he experienced at the Parson's home did not compare with what he was about to witness. A man unrecognizable lay in a bed with a tube entering his nose and a small plastic tube fastened to his arm.

He stood there and listened to the sounds of a machine which sounded like a slow drum beat as a man was being led to a wall by a firing squad. Chad watched him lying in bed, helpless and innocent. The thought revisited Chad's idea of the mistaken identity of Junior being in the wrong place at the wrong time.

The creak of the door caused Chad to turn around. A lady dressed in a green smock entered the room, walked up to the bed, and examined a transparent bag hanging from a chrome pole.

"Hello, my name is Karen." "Do you know him?"

"Yes, I am a co-worker, answering with a muffled voice. Do you know what happened to him?"

"No, I am sorry; all I know is he is in critical condition with a punctured lung.?

"Will he be okay?" asked Chad.

"Only time will tell. We have excellent surgeons. But we must remember, it is God who makes the final decision."

Chad left the room with a crushed spirit. Guilt overwhelmed him and the question of why God would allow this to happen raced through his mind.

The puzzle began to take shape, but the question of why Denton chose to attack Junior hung in the balance.

Stone radioed Romano from his cruiser and gave Romano directions to Denton's residence.

"What is this all about, Stone?"

"It is suspected Denton assaulted a man at Dixie's. It might be the break we needed. I will fill you in at Denton's place. Go north out of town on County Road 300 East for two miles, then turn on 400 North for three miles. Cross a bridge, and you will see me parked along the road."

"Roger that."

Romano arrived, and Stone updated him on what had happened at Dixie's.

The men cautiously turned into the driveway with their guns unholstered in the event of resistance. The home looked like a fortress with a tall white picket fence shielding the front and sides of the house. To the left of the driveway lay a beautiful pond. Weeping willows surrounded half the circumference of the pond and a pier with a rowboat bobbing in the water tied to the dock.

The cruisers pulled up in front of the house and sat surveying the window curtains for signs of life.

Romano cracked his door and tried to get out, but suddenly a large dog came from around the corner of the garage. Romano pulled his door shut and the dog leaped at Romano's car window with snarling teeth.

A man came from around the back of the house dressed in a plaid long-sleeved shirt carrying a heavy-duty dog leash.

"Come, here, Timber," as the man slapped his thighs.

The threat of being eaten alive ended when the man fastened the leash onto the dog's collar and took him into the house.

"Okay, who are you guys?"

The Feds flashed their I.D.s.

"Are you Crowley Denton, owner of "Nucleus Inc?"

"Yes, I am one of the owners. So what's this all about?"

"We will ask the questions."

"Who is the other owner, and where can we find him."

"Luke Martin, but he lives at 300 Sedgely Road."

Romano turned to Stone and asked him to get Martin since he knew the roads better than Romano did.

"Denton, we want you to come with us to the county headquarters for further questioning."

"Lean against the car so we can frisk you," ordered Higgins.

Denton had no weapons so they placed his hands behind his back and cuffed him. The severity of Bill Bradley's punctured lung and blood loss sealed his fate. The hospital called Romano on his car phone to update the news of Bradley's passing.

# A CHRISTMAS HOMECOMING

A remarkable event took place in Stocker on Christmas Eve. First, the silence of heavy snowflakes fell, blanketing everything under its path. The community had drifts up to three feet high with blowing gusts of wind.

It had been several months since the assault on Amos Parsons, but it did not deter Millie from having a spirit of Christmas. Millie and Becky bundled up in two layers of clothes and trampled through snow drifts to cut down a five-foot pine they had seen in the fall.

The previous Christmas, Becky had trimmed the tree, but it looked like a Charlie Brown Christmas tree. The upper part had festive, colorful lights, while the bottom contained assorted bulbs with no pattern.

Millie vowed she would give Becky a second chance next year.

Millie had finished taking a peach pie out of the oven and placing it on her baker's rack when she heard a crash from down the hallway.

"What happened, Becky?" as she ran into the living room.

"Oh, I dropped a box of ornaments off the top shelf of the closet, but nothing broke, I hope!"

Becky answered with fingers- crossed behind her back. The box had only two broken bulbs.

Millie sat in her rocking chair and thought of how much they had depended on Amos daily and his absence on the most incredible day of the year, Jesus' birthday; he would not be home. She reached over to the side table and clutched her Bible.

She turned to the book of Luke, Chapter two, when suddenly Millie could hear screeching down the hall.

"What on earth are you doing now, Rebecca Mae!" Millie cried out.

"The box of lights and ornaments are too heavy for me to pick up, so I am sliding them to the living room. Mom, please have patience with me. I am doing the best I can." Becky responded in a tearful sob.

Millie jumped from her rocker and rushed to Becky's aid.

"I am so sorry, honey, please forgive me."

Millie picked up the box, and Becky grabbed a smaller container and sat them down on the floor by the tree.

Millie watched as Rebecca decorated the tree and wondered if the Parson home would recover from the tragedy they had suffered.

"Mommy, let's pray daddy will get out of the hospital tomorrow?" as she hugged her mother.

Millie sat back down in her rocker while Becky climbed into her lap. They prayed God would make Christmas the best it could ever be.

Amos lay in his bed staring out his fifth-story window at the snowcapped trees. His mind wandered back to past Christmas' when Becky had been a toddler. One year she reached the bottom branches of the tree and proceeded to pull off a bulb and toss it across the room.

"Mr. Amos, are you awake?' asked Anita, the day nurse. "I have good news for you!"

"Now, what good news could you possibly bring me?" answered a frustrated Amos.

"I guess you're not interested in going home, huh?" smiled Anita.

"Are you serious, in this blizzard? What about the snow?" the doubting Thomas answered.

"We have a special sleigh with eight tiny reindeer under the hood which can glide over any snowdrift God places before us." a reassuring Anita answered.

"I will get a message to the doctor and see if we can get you out, pronto."

Amos settled back in his bed with his heart racing with excitement, but the happiness fled, and fear overcame him.

*How would Millie accept his wounded body? With the scarred face? The scarred nose? Would she shun a kiss from him or refuse to interlock her fingers with the few fingers he had left?*

*I am a mess.*

Anita came in with the discharge papers and home instructions for Amos.

"Okay, Mr. Amos, all you have to do is put an "X" on the highlighted line and follow two instructions from Dr. Fitzgerald. First, do not overdo it; secondly, make sure you use the cream I give you on your burned areas. I will be back to assist you in getting dressed if you need help and here is a coat you can wear till you get home."

It began to snow again, and the winter air had a frigid bite. The winds increased to thirty-five miles per hour with continued drifting snow.

They loaded Amos into the rear of the hospital van and strapped his wheelchair in securely.

Once they got out of the city limits, the snow became more of a challenge. However, the driver had an enormous determination to see the joy on the faces of the Parsons.

The driver had to speed up to push through the heavy snow in Parsons's driveway.

How on earth could one get excited over a four-foot-tall mailbox? But Amos did as he saw through the slits of his bandages

The moment of truth had arrived. Millie finished the lunch dishes when she heard a car door shut.

There was no path shoveled to the front door. Three feet of snow would be a trick to push out of the way without their patient freezing to death.

"Daddy's home! Daddy's home!" Becky hollered.

The men struggled to the rear of the van but realized it would be impossible to push a wheelchair in the deep snow.

Millie ran to the door and opened it.

"Wait I will get you a shovel." Millie yelled in excitement. She disappeared for a few minutes, then returned and pitched a shovel to the men, but it fell short of the van.

Jim and Don took turns shoveling the wet, heavy snow as the other waited in the van to stay warm. Becky and her mom watched from the picture window as each shovel of snow tossed from the path would be altered by the raging crosswinds.

The weary men cleared a path to the bottom stoop of the stairs and headed back to the van to get their cargo. Amos looked like a mummy from the Egyptian dynasty with blankets binding him from head to toe. They lowered the wheelchair down to the ground and began the tedious task of dragging the wheeled chair through the swathe they had shoveled. Millie shoveled the front porch off so she could help Amos into the house.

The scene of angels in heaven and the hallelujah chorus playing could not compare to the grand arrival of Amos coming into the home.

One of the attendants closed the door while Millie and the other man began unwrapping the best Christmas present Millie could have ever received. Then, finally, the final blanket came off, and Amos squinted his eyes so he could adjust to the light.

Mollie tentatively handled Amos's body like you would a porcelain doll. She placed her arms around his neck and softly kissed his neck.

"Mrs. Parson's, he is guaranteed not to break," smiled Jim.

Becky stood amazed at her daddy.

"Here is a tube of cream to apply to his skin daily," as Don pulled it out of a bag.

"And if you would be so kind as to sign the form for his safe delivery, we can join our family for Christmas Eve," Jim asked.

"Yes, sir," Millie answered as she took the form and pen from him.

One of the men reached for the doorknob and the men went onto the porch, turned back, and wished the Parson's a Merry Christmas.

Millie bent down, cradled Amos' head to her bosom, and began to pray: *Thank you, Lord, for bringing my husband home and answering our prayers.*

"Amos, I made a peach pie." Would you like a slice?" Millie asked as she kissed him on the forehead.

"I would love it." Amos answered, sporting a big grin.

"Becky, you can wheel daddy into the kitchen while I get the plates on the table," Millie said in haste.

They sat for the first time in months as a family. Mollie cut the pie and placed a slice on each plate. Millie watched tentatively on how her husband would eat the pie with fingers missing on each hand. Amos prayed, cautiously using his fork to cut a wedge of the pie and put it into his mouth. Part of the pie returned harmlessly to his plate on his first attempt.

"Amos, may I ask you a question?" Millie asked in an uneasy tone.

"Sure, what is it, honey," Amos replied.

"Well, while you were lying in the hospital, you had a visitor. Do you remember?"

"Why, no, who could it have been?" Amos answered with a puzzled look.

A man named Chad Henderson. The nurse told me he felt responsible for your injuries. How would you feel if I invited him and his family to visit you?" Millie asked.

"I think it would be great," Amos nodded with approval.

Millie made the necessary arrangements for the Henderson family to come over on Christmas Day.

A nervous feeling came over Chad when he got the news of the invitation from Mrs. Parson; he believed in leaving what happened to Parson's family paid in full.

"Don't you care about the damage done to the family, Chad?" Cindy asked in frustration.

"Well, sure I do, but I can't undo what has happened!" Chad responded.

"No, but God can do mighty things if you would only allow Him. Chad remained silent but agreed to visit the Parsons'.

Millie had baked chocolate chip cookies. Finally, the time had arrived for Chad to face Mr. Parsons and his family.

Christmas Day would be remembered forever by both families.

Chad meandered through the snow-covered roads, and as he came down Parson's road, he began to have flashbacks of the night of the fire. He became nervous as he pulled into their driveway.

Amos' favorite spot was to sit next to the Christmas tree, so he could watch the bird feeders out his front window.

"Millie, they are here," he yelled to her in the kitchen.

Chad got out of the car, and the Hendersons struggled to the front porch through the snow.

Chad and Cindy reached the top of the stairs and stomped the snow off their feet.

"Hello folks, please come in, and you can put your coats and boots behind the door.

"Sit down wherever you want. We had finished our devotions. Amos held out his hand to Chad in friendship, but Chad took one look at Amos's hand and dropped his arm to his side.

"I don't blame you, Mr. Henderson; my body is a mess," trying to put Chad at ease.

They huddled in the living room and made their introductions with added small talk. Millie suggested it would be better to move into the kitchen, where snacks and beverages would be better served.

She set up a card table in the living room and turned on the TV so the girls could be alone while they had their milk and cookies.

Millie placed some toys she had when Rebecca was a child and placed them on the floor for Joshua to play with, but he cried when Cindy put him down. Cindy had no choice but to hold him at the kitchen table.

Millie served everyone a piece of peach pie and coffee.

Cindy tapped Chad on his knee under the table to talk to Amos and Millie. Chad looked at her and turned to Amos and Millie.

"It's easy to accept an apology from someone when you know you are hurt, but to reverse the matter and know you were wrong and confess it to God and find the words to say to someone you hurt is difficult. When I followed in the parade in front of your home, I knew I had made a mistake. I had a grudge but held it against innocent people. I want you both to see I am so sorry for my participation and the injuries I brought to your family.

"Will you forgive me?" Chad asked with a tear visible on his cheek.

"Chad, would you move your chair over by me?" Amos asked.

"Chad, you know there had been a fight at Fisk's market before the cross burning. Mr. Fisk had threatened to do me bodily harm, and the Stocker police heard him make the threat. So, Chad, it would have happened whether you were there or not. For me to not forgive you would make me no better than the person who lit the fire in our front yard."

Chad looked surprised at Amos and reached out his hand in friendship.

Amos changed the subject as he felt Chad needed to process what he had shared with Chad.

On Christmas Day, Chad left his pride at the home of Amos Parsons and God began to work on his heart.

On Christmas Day, Chad learned the practical reason for Christmas, and an example of true forgiveness demonstrated by a man of a different color.

# A NEW CREATION

There is a time and place for everything. Pastor Keen called Chad and learned Chad and Cindy were going on a weekend trip to relax from the tension they had endured.

Chad asked the Pastor why he wanted to see him. Pastor Keen replied he could see a great deal of promise in him. Chad was flattered.

The Pastor told him he wanted to take him out to lunch and get better acquainted. A free meal did the trick in satisfying Chad's curiosity. He promised he would meet with him the following Saturday.

"Miracles are true after all," Cindy thought to herself as he entered the car. "Maybe it's spring, and good times are coming."

Cindy had a promise of her own. The man of God advised Cindy to stop nagging Chad about going to church. She reluctantly agreed but did not understand the reasoning of his suggestions.

The Pastor frequented several places throughout Stocker to study for the Sunday services. He decided John's diner would be the best for privacy. The restaurant would be close to Chad's and wouldn't be as crowded.

Saturday morning began with stormy weather with high winds and torrential rains. Pastor Keen arrived early to make sure the table in the diner's back would be available.

Fifteen minutes later, Chad arrived, and the waitress directed him to the rear of the restaurant.

"Bonnie, I would like you to meet my friend Chad."

"Oh, come on, Pastor, how can I live up to such a high reputation as that?" smiled Bonnie.

Here are two menus, and what can I get you guys to drink?" She took their orders and left.

"Well, Chad, you order anything you want. My treat. Oh, by the way, I prefer to be called Ed." Chad shook his head slightly in confusion. He believed anyone who did something for nothing wanted something in return.

"Listen, Chad, I didn't invite you here to pre-judge you for your past. I put my pants on like you – one leg at a time. My family seldom, if ever, went to church, except once being invited to a church Christmas play. In my senior year of high school, my life changed dramatically. A girl who moved to Stocker from Illinois invited me to a church youth outing at a roller-skating rink.

"You should have seen me on skates- disastrous."

Bonnie returned to the table with the drinks.

"Are you ready to order," she asked.

The men gave her their order, and she left again.

"Ever witnessed a miracle, Chad?"

Chad gave him a look like a deer in the headlights and lowered his face.

He began to stir his drink with his straw but didn't look up.

Finally, Chad raised his head at eye level with Ed and meekly answered, "No."

Once again, Bonnie returned carrying a tray of food she placed at an adjoining table. She repeated the orders; "Chad, you get biscuits and gravy, and Pastor, you ordered eggs benedict. Enjoy, and if there is anything else, don't hesitate to call me."

"I pray at every meal Chad. I hope you don't mind. I am so thankful for the good and the bad.'

Chad shook his head in confusion.

"Ed, why would you be thankful for bad things?"

"I know it doesn't make sense, but the one hundred and forty-fifth Psalm reads: *even in the darkest times in our lives; we can praise God for His love and promise to be near us.*

For the first time, Pastor Keen noticed a positive reaction from Chad. The Pastor prayed and then asked if he could ask Chad, another question.

"Sure, Ed, I am listening."

"You know everyone will die sometime. When we die, our spirit will go to one of two places: Heaven or Hell.

Chad looked down at his food and seemed preoccupied with stirring his food with his fork.

"Do you know where you will spend eternity, Chad?"

Chad raised his head from his plate and, with a soft meek answer, "answered "no."

"Would you like me to tell you how you can know?" Ed asked

A small tear began to leak from his good eye and the miracle happened.

"He nodded his head in affirmative action. The transforming miracle took place in Chad's life.

He asked Cindy to be seated with him at the kitchen table.

"What's the matter, Chad! Is something wrong?" fear radiating from her body.

Chad reached to a bowl at the center of the kitchen table and grabbed a piece of hard candy from a bowl, and unwrapped it.

"Will you go with me to church on Sunday?" Chad asked. Cindy leaped from her seat and ran around the table, and wrapped her arms around Chad's neck.

"Yes! Yes! Chad, Yes!"

The church bells rang Sunday morning, and Chad smiled at the thought it was the first time he had heard them.

The family loaded up in the car and drove to Victory Church.

The trees had their green foliage and the streets were washed clean – It was as if God had plans to renew everything with the previous night's storm. Cindy smiled cheek to cheek. She still couldn't believe the magic which happened last night.

Chad parked in the church parking lot and Cindy got the kids out of the car and began walking to the church. Cindy turned back to see if Chad was coming.

Cindy met her mother at the front door, and Verna took the kids to their classrooms.

"What's the matter, Cindy?"

"Oh, it's Chad. I am going back to the car and see what is wrong."

She walked back to the car and reached her hand through the open window and placed her hand on his shoulder.

"Hey honey, what is wrong?" a concerned Cindy asked as she stood by the car.

"It's been so long, Cindy; I just don't feel right; what if God doesn't accept me?"

"His Graciousness is accepting; it seeks people like us, and embraces us into its massive arms of mercy," a consoling Cindy answered.

"Are you sure?"

"Yes, I'm sure! He wouldn't have let you drive us here if he didn't want you inside."

"I've wronged so many people in so many ways?"

"But you repented, right? When you met with Pastor Keen."

"Yes, I did." "That's everything; God loves those who repent of their sins and those who confess their sin to Him. And you did." Cindy lovingly explained to Chad.

Cindy opened the door and put her arm around his neck; Chad lifted his head and climbed out of the car. They walked to the church; Cindy still had her arm wrapped around his waist.

They reached the entrance, and Cindy let go of Chad. Chad grasped her hand as they set foot inside the church. The two walked the aisle as Cindy remembered her wedding day. She was beaming, and the warmth of Chad's grip traversed through her very soul.

"I love you," she whispered as the two made their way to a pew. Chad nodded to the Pastor as he sat down.

Pastor Keen stepped to the pulpit. "Everyone here in this church, including me, has a tendency to err. We are all sinners" he began.

The murmuring settled, and people listened.

"We are God's creation."

Chad looked up as Pastor Keen continued.

Pastor Keen continued with the sermon and occasionally glanced at Chad and Cindy.

The crowd listened intently as Pastor Keen continued.

Finally, the pastor closed.

"Miracles are true after all," Cindy thought to herself as they met her mother and kids at the front door.

"It's spring, and good times are coming...."

# A TIME OF REFLECTION

"Work is never done for a mother. Cindy had the children settled at the kitchen table while she prepared breakfast. She decided to let Chad sleep in on Saturday morning since he had been working overtime at the factory. She began to butter the toast for Brooke when the phone rang.

"Hello, Oh, hello, pastor. Yes, he is sleeping, but it's time for him to get up."

"Chad, it's for you; the pastor is on the phone!"

"Tell him I'll be there in a minute," a droopy-eyed Chad replied, still lazily folded in his blanket.

"Hello Pastor."

"Let me ask Cindy."

He wants to pick me up in an hour.

"What about taking the kids to the movie? We promised them." Cindy pleaded.

"Can't we take in the last matinee, honey?"

"Oh, sure. I forgot there is another movie."

"Okay, pastor, I will be ready. Bye."

To no one's surprise, a newborn baby cannot eat a thick succulent sirloin steak smothered in onions. So, it is with a person who has lived their entire life with greed to get whatever it takes to bring happiness: money, prestige, power, or the toys of a person has to grow into a different way of thinking: taking baby steps to maturity.

Pastor Keen's task with mentoring and teaching Chad had only begun. Chad's childhood had been glorious, but he had a more significant responsibility. God had given him a family to shepherd, just as a pastor of a church body.

The plan by Pastor Keen for the next several months was to work with Chad weekly to help improve his family's leadership.

Cindy greeted the pastor at the front door; then, she hollered to the bathroom door to see if Chad could hear the question she wanted to ask the pastor. He did not respond.

"Pastor, what's got into him? I cannot believe he's the same man who became agitated when you mentioned the word "church" in a sentence."

"Cindy," Ed answered in his usual humble and preaching tone. "God has his ways, and one of his ways is to teach with patience and let the Holy Spirit do the work.

Chad had come out of the bathroom and joined Cindy and the pastor.

"Okay, I am ready," hugging Cindy and kissing her.

"Hey, what about me?" a small voice came from the kitchen.

"Excuse me, I'll be right back."

"I have someone calling me." winked Chad.

Imagine the beauty of the first garden of Eden with its water supply and the spacious vegetation it provided to man's eyes.

One of the paradoxes in Stocker Community church has been the work of a few laymen to recreate the Garden of Eden in the back of the church. The element of surprise would overwhelm Chad as the pastor pulled his auto behind the rear parking lot of the parish.

"I don't believe what I am seeing,' exclaimed Chad. "It is like a state park you would visit in Ohio."

The grounds were spacious, with lush green grass surrounding an octagon gazebo roofed with shingles and a picnic table centered under the roof. In the background was a row of trees with a comprehensive stream.

"Do you know what your seeing is to represent, Chad? "

"Why, no, what is it?" a puzzled look came over Chad's face.

"It is to picture a replica of the Garden of Eden in our finite minds."

The pastor reached into the back seat and grabbed a black leather-bound Bible with Chad's name engraved on the front of the cover.

He handed it to Chad and told him to open the cover.

Chad obeyed, and to Chad's amazement were the words inscribed: *TO CHAD FROM STOCKER COMMUNITY CHURCH. OCTOBER 12, 1969.*

"What does the date mean, pastor?" asked Chad inquisitively.

"That is the date you received Jesus in your heart," Ed answered.

"Chad, the Bible is God's marching orders for His people, as he patted Chad's shoulder. So don't let it gather dust on the cover, but read it."

"So now, let's walk to the gazebo in the middle of the yard and bring your Bible." smiled Ed.

"The gospel of St. John is where I am starting. Why? New converts need the reassurance of God's love and the importance of sharing the love in Word and deed. People do not care how much you know but want to know how much you care." The pastor kept the study brief as Chad needed to spend Saturday with his family.

Chad returned home with a glow on his face. He was the happiest man in the universe.

Cindy met the men in the driveway and Chad showed her his new Bible.

"It's beautiful, Chad."

"See you tomorrow" Ed said, as he backed out of the driveway.

"Okay, Cindy, what time is the matinee?" Chad asked enthusiastically.

"Well, the Adventures of Huckleberry Finn is on the 3:30 matinee, and then if you want, we can go out for pizza, hummm Chad? hmmm, Chad. Oh, by the way, mother agreed to babysit Joshua."

"Sounds great to me." Chad smiled with a raised hand.

# TRIAL OF THE DECADE

Chad received a phone call Tuesday evening from Romano asking him if he could come down to headquarters. Chad, puzzled by the request, agreed.

"What's the phone call about?" asked Cindy, worried her husband might be in trouble again.

The police did not say, but I best cooperate with them," Chad answered exasperatedly.

The clerk at the desk led Chad to a conference room and told him someone would be right in. The room looked ordinary, but Chad noticed a large black curtain on one of the walls. Romano and Higgins entered a few minutes later. Higgins walked up to the same wall and pulled back the curtain.

"Look through the window Chad, and what do you see?" asked Romano.

"I see five men standing in a row with a number attached to the front of their coat," Chad responded, astonished.

"Very good. I want you to study each man and identify them as being the men sitting at the table that night." Romano commanded.

Chad sifted through each man and gave the numbers three and five.

"You are sure, Chad, number three and number five?"

"Yes, those were the men at the table Friday night.

"Now, I want you to sit down. I have some awful news for you."

Chad sat down, and Romano placed his hand on his shoulder. He was struggling to say what he had to do next.

"Your friend, you know as Junior, passed away earlier today. I am sorry."

A chill ran down Chad's spine. He lowered his head into his hands and never said a word. The silence fell thick around him as he tried to process the devastating news.

*"Junior is gone?"* he thought, petrified. Then he finally said, "Junior had nothing to do with what I had done. So why did they single him out?" his voice cracked.

"We believe you were the one they wanted to kill. You may still be in danger but not by these men. They are in our custody."

"But by who?"

"We do not know yet. But, we will have your home under surveillance. So, tell only your wife."

"Thanks, Chad, you have been a big help. We will keep in touch."

Men do not cry. Chad's father told him when he walked out of Chad's life. It shows weakness. But the news of the loss of his best friend overwhelmed him with guilt. He felt responsible for his death.

The wheel of justice can be slow. It is more than a man dressed in black perched behind a desk pounding a black gavel on a piece of wood. The events leading to the possible arrests of Denton and Martin involved the Federal Government and the Stocker police.

Denton's charges of attempted murder and reckless endangerment were like catching the little fish in the pond. Moreover, the Feds had possession of Denton's white-handled knife with Junior's blood on the blade. Still, the obvious question of who masterminded the cross burning at the Parson home loomed the big question.

During the interrogation of the relationship between Denton and the store owner, Nelson Fisk, Romano learned Denton had married Fisk's daughter, Ruby Fisk.

The Circuit Judge agreed to a court order which gave Romano access to search "Nucleus Inc." and Martin and Denton's homes.

The knowledge of the assault on Parson at Fisk's store proved to be a valuable link to why the cross-burning occurred at Parson's house.

*"Could Fisk have been the mastermind behind the attack on Parson?"* Chad wondered.

The answers the Feds sought were of no importance to Chad. The walk to his car seemed to be a never-ending journey. The distance and time allotted from the precinct to his driveway had vanished in his mind. He shut the engine off and remained seated behind the steering wheel. The guilt consumed him. He finally put his head on the steering wheel and wept.

The scenic beauty of the trees changing colors from green to conspicuous shades of gold, orange, and red reminded him winter was on the horizon. The people of Stocker turned their attention to coon hunting every year during October and November, but this year would be different.

Sixty miles down the road, the most significant event in Ohio history since the state joined the union was about to begin. A chess match between two forces, good and evil; black versus white could change American history.

The elderly or shut-ins spend their time-solving puzzles, but the prosecution had a hill of their own finding the missing link.

*Squelch-Squelch* came the sound over Romano's car radio while he had Denton's business under surveillance. The reports, investigation, and researchers learned that "Nucleus Inc." had been a booming business owned by co-owners Luke Martin and Nelson Fisk's son-in-law, Crowley Denton. Finally, the G-men were able to connect the dots. Denton and Martin met during their enlistment in the Navy on a naval base near Asheville,

North Carolina. The company made parachutes used for cargo and supplies in support of Vietnam.

Nucleus Inc produced cloth material for vendors to be used on various products. The large building in a valley was surrounded by tall piness. There was only one entry visible from the highway.

Now the men had been arrested and were in custody the next objective was to visit Fisk's market. Two patrol cars blocked the front entrance while Romano and Higgins drove to the rear. Two men entered the store through the front door and called out Fisk's name. The men drew their weapons from their holsters, anticipating trouble.

Suddenly, the men could hear the sound of an engine from the rear of the store. They rushed back out to the front parking lot and opened fire on Fisk's car tires, causing the car to crash into a tree. Fisk got out of the car and tried to run, but one of the officer's gang tackled him.

Romano and Higgins knew the puzzle had one more piece missing. The last area to search would be the shack attached to the back of the store. The men pounded on the door and called for someone to come out. No response. Romano took his foot and kicked open the door. The only light came from the sunlight through the cracks in the wall.

The room contained a cot in the corner and a dresser on the other side of the wall. The room smelled of tobacco and urine. A loud noise startled the men on the opposite end of the shack.

They turned with guns drawn.

"Don't shoot, please don't shoot."

A dirty long-haired man stood with his arms raised.

"What's your name?" yelled Romano.

"Bill Crawford."

Higgins took him into custody while another officer and Romano searched the premises. A knife found by Crawford's cot and an 8x10 photograph of Cindy and Bill were confiscated and used as evidence.

Fisk, Denton, and Martin's charges were hate crimes, and Cindy's ex-boyfriend was charged with murder in the first degree.

An arraignment scheduled before the Judge at one o'clock in the afternoon would determine the men's fate. The trial did not just affect the Buckeyes but states as far away as Alabama. The press and media coverage would relentlessly add to the area's tension. In addition, the local businesses were preparing for the vast number of people coming in from the adjoining states.

In the courtyard outside of the Federal Court Building in Salisbury, the local law enforcement organized security in the event of a riot.

A black limousine stopped at the courthouse, and a tall, slender man got out of the car. He looked about forty-five years old with peppered black hair and sunglasses. Once entering the lobby, a press gathering approached him with microphones outstretched, trying to get news. Still, Hank Greenburgh, one of the defense attorneys, pushed his way to the elevator.

The prosecutor, Jake Simpson, stood on the fourth floor with two of his aids. The ding of the elevator door opened and caught Simpson's attention bringing eye contact with his counterpart, Greenburgh.

With a smirk, Greenburgh walked up to Simpson and said, "Well, Big Buff.

"What do you hope to gain charging these men with roughing up a negro?"

Simpson never said a word but turned and walked down the hall to the first door to the left and entered. He delivered one of two manilla envelopes he carried and laid it on the counter.

"Hello, Buford," replied the court secretary, "everything in order?"

"Now, Mrs. Smith, you need not ask a question like that!" with an extreme arrogance in his voice.

The trial concluded the case of Crowley and Martin. Each man received five years in prison. However, Fisk's punishment was more severe. He received ten years in the pen and a ten thousand dollar fine on Amos Parson's behalf.

Bill Crawford received the maximum the judge was allowed.

The circumstance warranted a sentence of death by the state of Ohio.

Chad Henderson learned two valuable lessons about revenge in his life. First, God never allows sin to go unpunished and, leaves all the circumstance's in one's life to be decided by God and at His chosen time.

www.ingramcontent.com/pod-product-compliance
Lightning Source LLC
LaVergne TN
LVHW040200080526
838202LV00042B/3253